Great Start!

**Purchased with
Smart Start Funds**

HIDE~AND~SEEK WORD BIRD

by Jane Belk Moncure
illustrated by Linda Sommers Hohag

THE CHILD'S WORLD

MANKATO, MN 56001

Library of Congress Cataloging in Publication Data

Moncure, Jane Belk.
  Hide-and-seek Word Bird.

  (Word Birds for early birds)
  Summary: Uses simple vocabulary to depict
Word Bird's game with Papa.
  [1. Hide-and Seek—Fiction]   I. Hohag,
Linda, ill.   II. Title.   III. Series: Moncure,
Jane Belk.   Word Birds for early birds.
PZ7.M739Hi   [E]   81-18068
ISBN 0-89565-218-8 -1991 Edition   AACR2

HIDE~AND~SEEK WORD BIRD

"Let's play hide-and-
seek," said Word Bird.

Papa closed his eyes.
Word Bird hid.

"One, two, three. Here
I come," said Papa.

Papa looked

under
the
chair,

and under the rug.

Papa looked all
around the living room.

"Where are you,
Word Bird?

"There you are.

Under
the
couch."

"It is my turn," said Papa. Word Bird closed his eyes. Papa hid.

"One, two, three. Here I come."

Word Bird looked behind the clock,

and behind
the
door.

Word Bird looked all
around the dining room.

"Where are you,
Papa?

"There you are.

Behind the cupboard."

"Let me play," said Mama.

Papa and Word Bird
closed their eyes.
Mama hid.

"One, two, three. Here
we come."

Papa and Word Bird
looked behind the stove,

and under the sink.

They looked all
around the kitchen.

"Where are you, Mama?

"There you are.

Under
the
table."

"Now it is time for bed," said Papa.

"Just one more time?" asked Word Bird.

"One more time," said Papa.

Mama and Papa
closed their eyes.
Word Bird hid.

"One,
two,
three.
Here
we
come."

Mama and Papa looked

in the closet,

and behind
the dresser.

They looked all
around the bedroom.

"Where are you,
Word Bird?"

Then they peeked
into Word Bird's room.

Guess where Word Bird was? He was in his own bed, fast asleep.

You can read these Word Bird words.

chair

rug

cupboard

couch

stove

sink

clock

door

table

bed

closet